# Broken Wings Will Fly

By Mick Blackistone
Illustrated by Jennifer Heyd Wharton

Tidewater Publishers
Centreville, Maryland

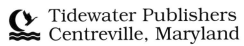

For Mattie Linn Bowie,
with thanks for her
inspiration and courage,
and for other children
with disabilities,
with the hope that they
will encounter fair winds
and following seas
throughout life

FROM high on top of the hill, Sally could watch all of the activity on the water during the summer months. She looked down and saw the sailboats slowly cruising along, the powerboats pulling the waterskiers, the fishermen coming and going through the inlet searching for fish in the ocean waters beyond; and she watched her friends racing their small sailboats around a course of buoys set up for them to practice for the big race weekend that would take place at the end of the summer.

When there were not many people out on the water, Sally loved to watch all the ducks and seagulls flying and soaring over the water. "They are so beautiful and so free," she said to her dog Tucker as he sat calmly beside her. "And they seem so very happy, too."

Sally knew that the people, including her friends, using the water were happy and she thought the seabirds and Tucker were always happy too. But Sally was not happy. She was not happy at all because of the car accident she'd been in last year.

The accident with the pickup truck happened one night when she and her mother were driving home from a school fair. Her mother was not hurt, and the driver of the other car was only slightly injured, but Sally was hurt very badly. Now she could not move her legs and must use a wheelchair to go from place to place. The doctor told her mother that she would never be able to walk again. Even after leaving the hospital and working with physical therapists, to make her muscles stronger and movements easier, she was sad and angry. She was sad because she couldn't race her sailboat or run or ride bikes with her friends anymore. She was angry because she was the one who got hurt and she didn't think that was fair.

When her mother talked about going down to watch the boat races or the children practicing for race weekend, Sally would always say the same thing: "Not today; I don't feel like it. I'll sit here in this stupid wheelchair and watch everyone else have fun." This made her mother feel sad.

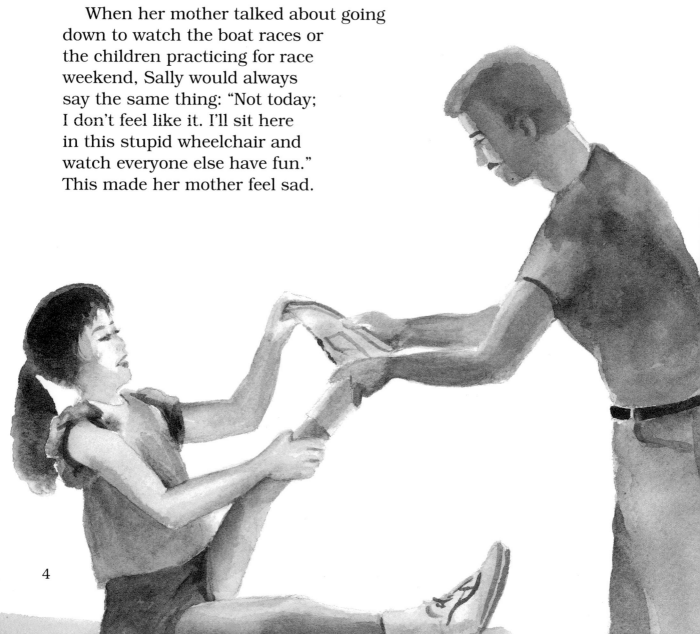

4

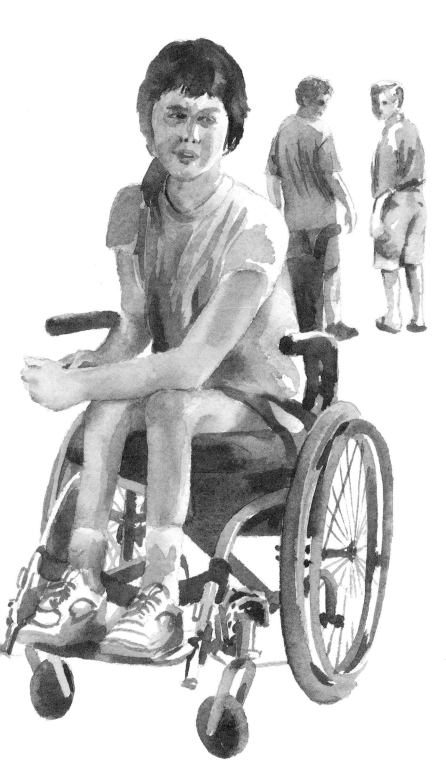

One day a few weeks later, Sally's friends, Bobby and Tommy, stopped by to see her. "Come on down to the boathouse. We're getting ready for the big race weekend and you can visit while we clean up the place and start practicing," Tommy said.

"Yeah," said Bobby. "You're a better sailor than all of us. Come on down and help us out."

"No way," Sally said. "I'm not going to the boathouse. I'm not a sailor anymore and I don't want to help you get ready for the big race weekend. I'm stuck in this wheelchair. And besides, I'll only get in the way since I can't do anything. Why don't you just leave and go do your boat work without me."

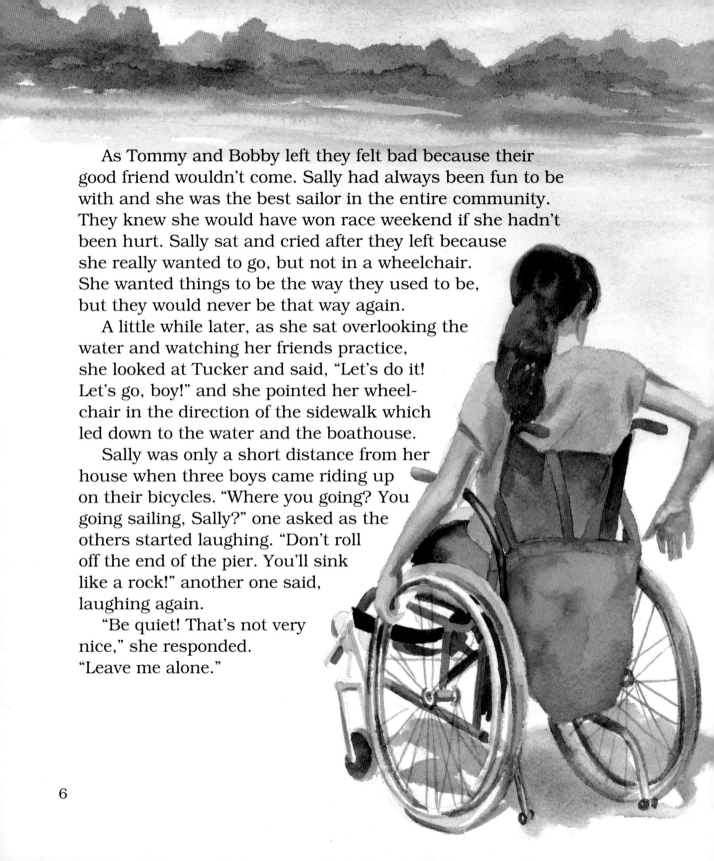

As Tommy and Bobby left they felt bad because their good friend wouldn't come. Sally had always been fun to be with and she was the best sailor in the entire community. They knew she would have won race weekend if she hadn't been hurt. Sally sat and cried after they left because she really wanted to go, but not in a wheelchair. She wanted things to be the way they used to be, but they would never be that way again.

A little while later, as she sat overlooking the water and watching her friends practice, she looked at Tucker and said, "Let's do it! Let's go, boy!" and she pointed her wheelchair in the direction of the sidewalk which led down to the water and the boathouse.

Sally was only a short distance from her house when three boys came riding up on their bicycles. "Where you going? You going sailing, Sally?" one asked as the others started laughing. "Don't roll off the end of the pier. You'll sink like a rock!" another one said, laughing again.

"Be quiet! That's not very nice," she responded. "Leave me alone."

"Okay," one of them said. "But you're stupid if you think you're going to do anything but roll around in that wheelchair—unless you want to try and chase us on our bikes. You might do that!" he said as the three rode off laughing.

Sally began crying again and even Tucker licking her face couldn't make her feel better. The boys had hurt her feelings and she felt terrible.

"Come on, Tucker. This was a bad idea. Let's go home and forget about going to the boathouse. I don't belong there anyway." And she cried as she pushed her wheelchair home.

When she reached her spot of grass on the hill in the backyard, Tucker immediately ran toward a group of trees at the edge of the yard. He started barking and running in small circles, stopping only to poke his nose into the leaves.

"What's going on, Tucker?" she yelled. "Stop that!" But Tucker kept barking and pointing with his nose to the ground.

"Okay, okay. Let me see what you've found, boy. There must be something there for you to get this excited." In fact, Tucker's excitement made her forget about the boys making fun of her as she went over to see what her dog was barking about.

As she approached the trees she saw a small duck nestled in the leaves and branches. The duck didn't move. He just sat very still as Tucker continued barking.

"Stop it, Tucker! It's a little duck. He's scared and it looks like he may be hurt. Be quiet! You're scaring him even more. Sit here. Sit!" Sally commanded. Tucker obeyed

her command and she edged
closer in her wheelchair to get
a better look.

"It's okay," she said softly to
the little duck. "Are you all right?
Let me see you." Very slowly she
moved a little closer and got into a
position where she could reach down
from her wheelchair and pet the wild bird.

"It's okay. Will you let me pet you?" Sally
asked the little duck as she reached down
and stroked its head feathers. The little
duck didn't move and after a few minutes
seemed comforted by Sally's touch and
soft voice.

Sally turned to Tucker who was
sitting patiently next to her. "Go
and get Mom. This little duck
is hurt. Go on. Go
get Mom." Tucker
barked and ran
for the house.

A few minutes later Sally's mother came running out. "What's the matter? Are you okay?" she asked. Sally put her finger to her lips, signaling for her mother to be quiet. As her mother approached and saw the duck, Sally said quietly, "He's hurt. I think his wing is broken. See how it lies to the side? We need to get him to the doctor." Her mother reached slowly for the duck and gently picked it up, cradling it against her chest. "Thattaboy. Everything will be fine now," her mother whispered to the duck. "Let's get you to the veterinarian and see how badly you've hurt yourself."

Soon they were off to the vet's office with the duck resting on a pillow on Sally's lap.

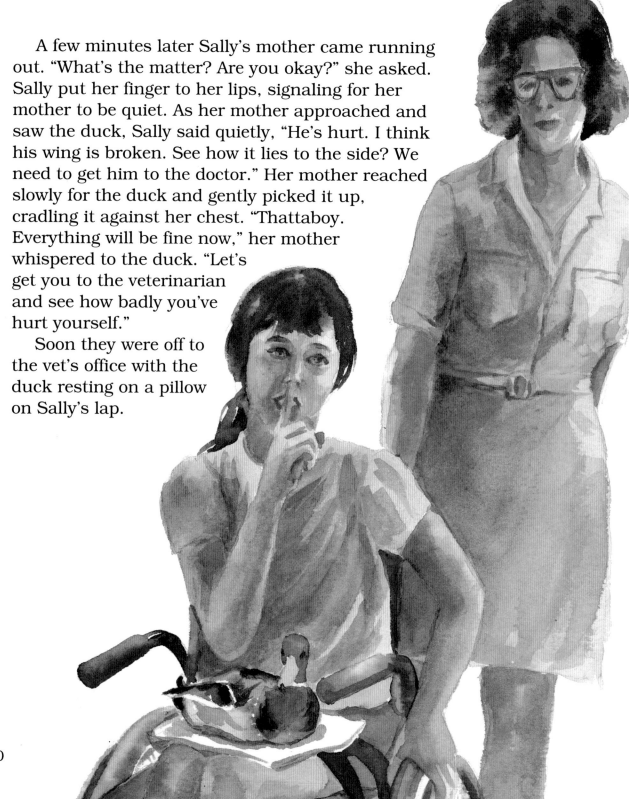

The veterinarian confirmed Sally's fears. The duck did have a broken wing. He would heal in time but would not be able to fly for several weeks. "You take care of him and make him comfortable," the doctor said. "He will be scared and he won't know what is happening to him. But I'm sure you and Tucker can handle this job."

"We will. We'll take good care of him and make him as happy as we can."

11

For the next few days the duck sat on his pillow next to Sally and Tucker overlooking the water. They watched the children practice for the big race weekend.

"Gosh, Tucker, I wish I were down there having fun. I know I could win the race but I'll never be able to do anything again except sit in this stupid wheelchair and watch everyone else. I'm glad that I have you to keep me company. At least you don't make fun of me. But you won't be here forever. Then what will I do?" Tucker looked into her eyes and looked at the duck with his broken wing. He walked over and softly licked the top of the little duck's head and then went over and gave Sally the same kind of kiss on her chin. She smiled and reached for the duck's pillow to carry him inside.

A few days later the injured duck began to squirm to his feet and step off the pillow to walk around the yard. His wing had not healed yet but he did walk a lot for exercise. Sally watched the little duck and Tucker walking around the big yard. She enjoyed their company very much and liked the way Tucker always seemed to push the little duck along.

"That little duck is working hard at getting better," her mother said one day. "It won't be long until he tries to flap his broken wing and realizes that he can fly out across the water again."

"Oh, Mom, he won't be able to do that for a long time. He was hurt very badly. He doesn't want to try too soon, you know," Sally responded.

"Well, we'll see. Let's hope he flies soon so he can be with the other ducks where he belongs," her mother said.

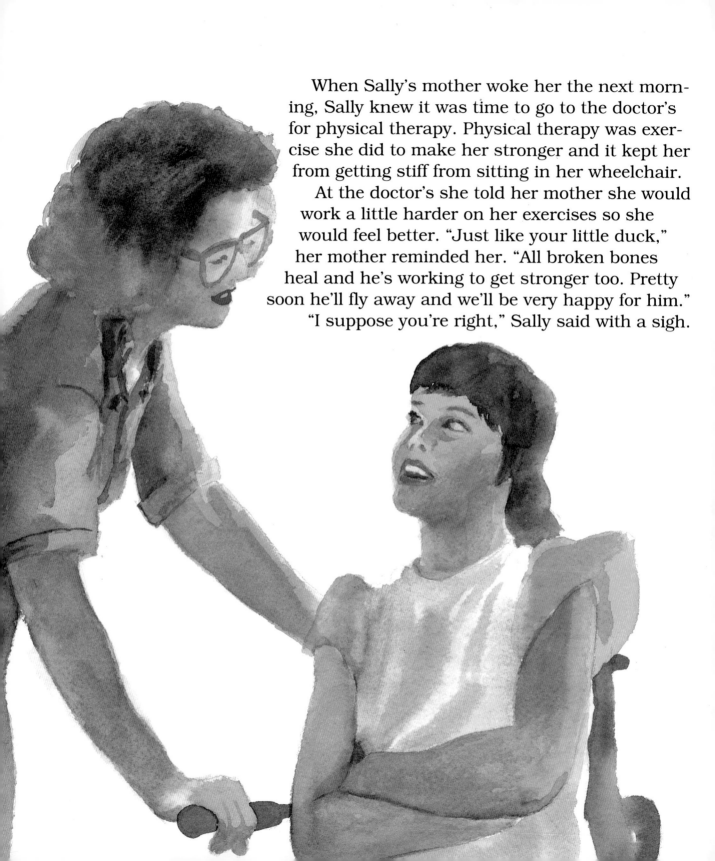

When Sally's mother woke her the next morning, Sally knew it was time to go to the doctor's for physical therapy. Physical therapy was exercise she did to make her stronger and it kept her from getting stiff from sitting in her wheelchair.

At the doctor's she told her mother she would work a little harder on her exercises so she would feel better. "Just like your little duck," her mother reminded her. "All broken bones heal and he's working to get stronger too. Pretty soon he'll fly away and we'll be very happy for him."

"I suppose you're right," Sally said with a sigh.

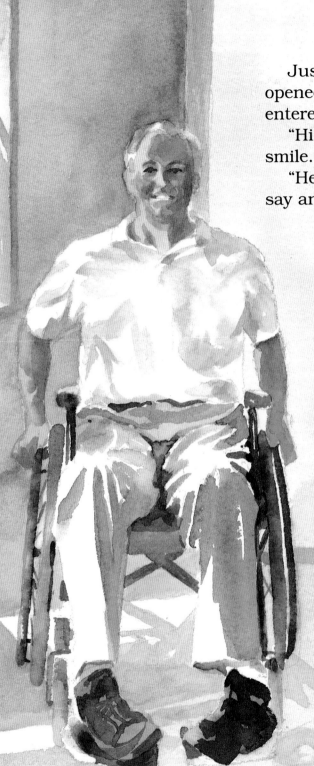

Just then the door to the doctor's office opened and a man about her father's age entered the room in his wheelchair.

"Hi," he said out loud and flashed a big smile.

"Hello," said Sally's mother. Sally didn't say anything.

"How are you doing? In for a few exercises?" he asked Sally with a grin.

"No, I can't do anything anymore except watch other people doing things I used to do!" she answered. "I used to sail my boat and ride my bike with my friends, but not anymore."

"What! You quit sailing? And quit riding your bike too? Well, who needs a bike? You have a wheelchair!" the man said enthusiastically.

"Sure, but it's not the same," Sally responded. "How did you get hurt anyhow?"

"Well, first of all, my name is John. I was shot in the Viet Nam war and I can't move my legs either. What's your name?"

"Sally."

Just then the nurse came to get Sally. As she was going through the door John spoke to her, "Hey, when are we going sailing?" and then she was gone.

15

A few days later Sally's mother had just finished helping her dress when there was a knock at the door. "Who could that be?" her mother wondered.

"I don't know," Sally replied. "All my friends are either practicing for the big race weekend or outside messing around."

When Sally and her mother went to answer the door they were surprised to see John, the man from the doctor's office, at the door.

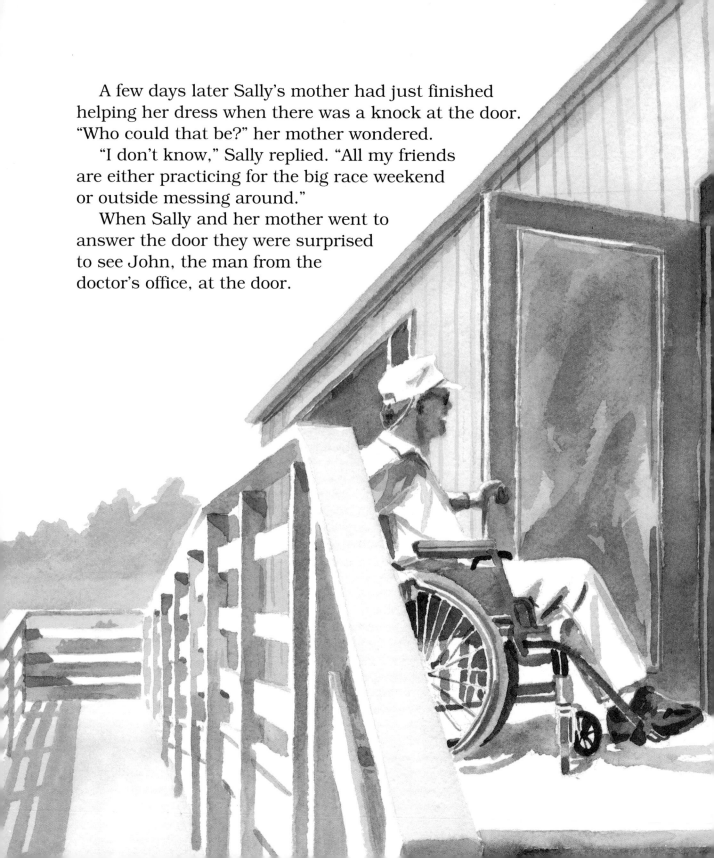

"Well, I see I didn't wake anyone up! Now, if it's okay with your mother, you and I are going sailing!"

"Sailing!" Sally exclaimed.

"Sure," John said. "My boat's down by the boathouse. It's all rigged for you and me with a few special gadgets to help with our disabilities, but other than that it's all sail-boat. And my friend Sam is there to be our able-bodied crew."

"No way. Not me!" Sally said. "I'm not going. That would be another reason for some of the kids to make fun of me. And besides, I can't do it anyway. What about this dumb wheelchair? I can't even get up, much less sail a boat!"

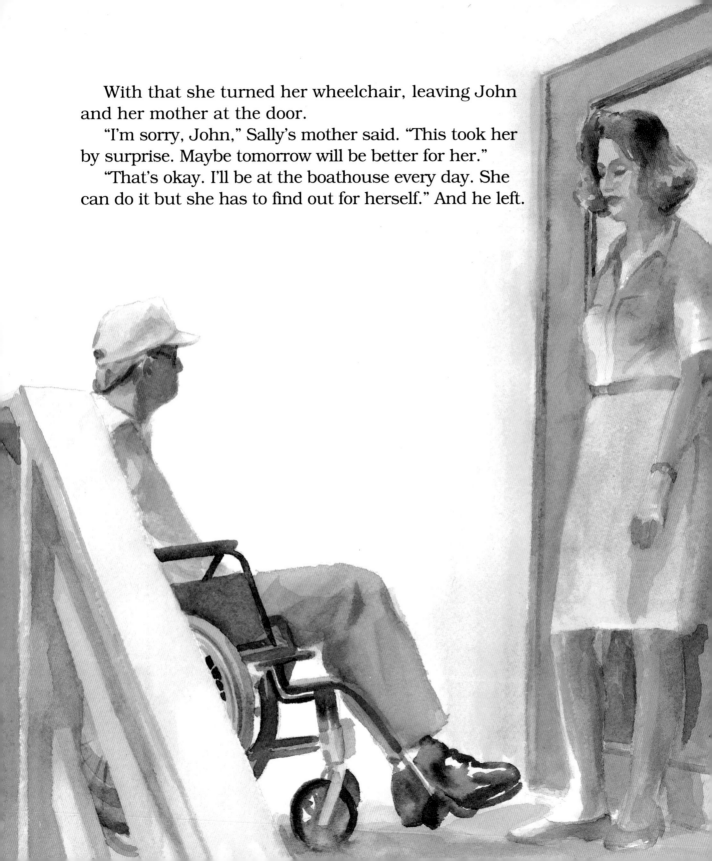

With that she turned her wheelchair, leaving John and her mother at the door.

"I'm sorry, John," Sally's mother said. "This took her by surprise. Maybe tomorrow will be better for her."

"That's okay. I'll be at the boathouse every day. She can do it but she has to find out for herself." And he left.

Meanwhile Sally sat in the backyard overlooking the water with Tucker and the little duck beside her. Every once in a while the little duck would startle her when he stood up to flap his broken wing. The little duck kept trying to fly and Sally and Tucker watched every time.

"Keep trying, boy. You'll get it. Don't quit, just rest awhile and then try again," she would say to the little duck. And a few minutes later the duck would try again.

Two days later the duck was making short flights across the yard about six feet off the ground. Sally would watch, then clap and cheer when the flights seemed better and better. Tucker showed his enthusiasm by running as fast as he could all around the little duck, barking and jumping.

On the third day the little duck flew across the yard and off the top of the hill. He flew out over the water, making a sweeping circle before coming back to land near Sally and Tucker. Minutes later he took off again and circled the water below. Then, as he came back in the direction of Sally's yard he flew up instead of down and circled high above the house, yard, and trees. Tucker barked and Sally waved excitedly. The little duck did not land. He flew down close to his new friends and back out over the inlet toward the coastline. He did not return.

Sally sat very still in her wheelchair. Tucker ran barking to the edge of the hilltop. As the little duck disappeared, Sally's eyes filled with tears. "He is free again, Tucker," she said. "His wing is better and he's gone. I'm going into the house to tell Mom. I don't want to stay out here anymore to-day."

Sally went into the house and told her mother that the little duck's wings were strong enough to fly and that he had flown away.

"Well, that little duck seemed to work on his broken wing until it became strong, and when he found out he could fly he wanted to go and be free again."

"I know, Mom, but I didn't think he would heal so quickly. He just kept trying and finally did it. And now he's gone and I miss him," Sally said.

"Of course you miss him, but aren't you glad that he's doing what he wants to do?" her mother asked.

"Yes," Sally responded. "But now I don't have him to keep me company with Tucker."

"Well, I have an idea that could take your mind off being lonely," her mother said. "You haven't wanted to go down to the pier to see John's boat, or any of your friends, so why don't we do that? He's a very nice man and he did invite you. It might be worth a try; come on."

"Well, okay," Sally said reluctantly. "I'll go and see it but I'm not sure that I'm going to go on it. I am in this wheel-chair, you know!"

Arriving at the water's edge, Sally could see that John's boat was not at the pier. As she left the special van her mother drove, she told her mother, "We should go. He's not here."

"Yes, he is!" her mother said as she pointed out beyond the end of the pier to a small sailboat moving in their direc-tion. John was at the tiller steering the boat toward Sally as her mother pushed her out on the wooden planks.

As the boat touched the end of the pier, John was quick to greet Sally. "Well, hello! I'm glad you decided to come down. Come on and go out with me. Wheel your chair over by that gadget at the end of the pier. Sam will help you from there, if you need it," John said.

Sally approached Sam, who was standing by a shiny wooden box which was about the same height as her wheelchair seat.

"This is what we call a transfer box," he said. "Move over beside it because this is how you're going to get aboard John's boat."

Sam smiled at Sally as he flipped the lid of the transfer box over and touched it to the side of John's boat, making a little ramp from the pier to the cockpit of the sailboat. Sally slowly edged herself into the transfer box and gently moved down the ramp into the cockpit, where she could slide off her chair into the specially designed pivoting seat. "Secure your seat belt just like you do in a car," John said with a smile. "And flip the transfer box lid up so we can cast off."

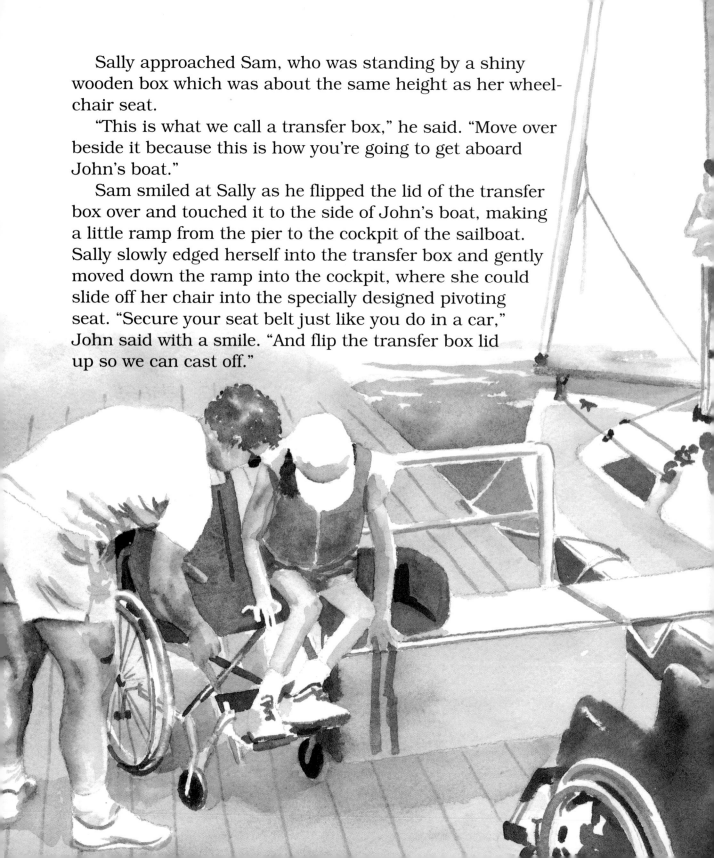

Once on board the sailboat, Sally was a little nervous, even though John was with her and she had her life jacket on and her seat belt fastened. She held tightly to the side of the boat as John steered away from the pier. Her mother was nervous too, but she smiled and waved. Sally gave her mother a short wave good-bye and her hand quickly returned to the security of the hold she had on the boat. "Relax now," John said. "This boat is specifically designed for people with disabilities like ours. It has a very heavy keel so it won't tip over and it's totally rigged for us to control it.

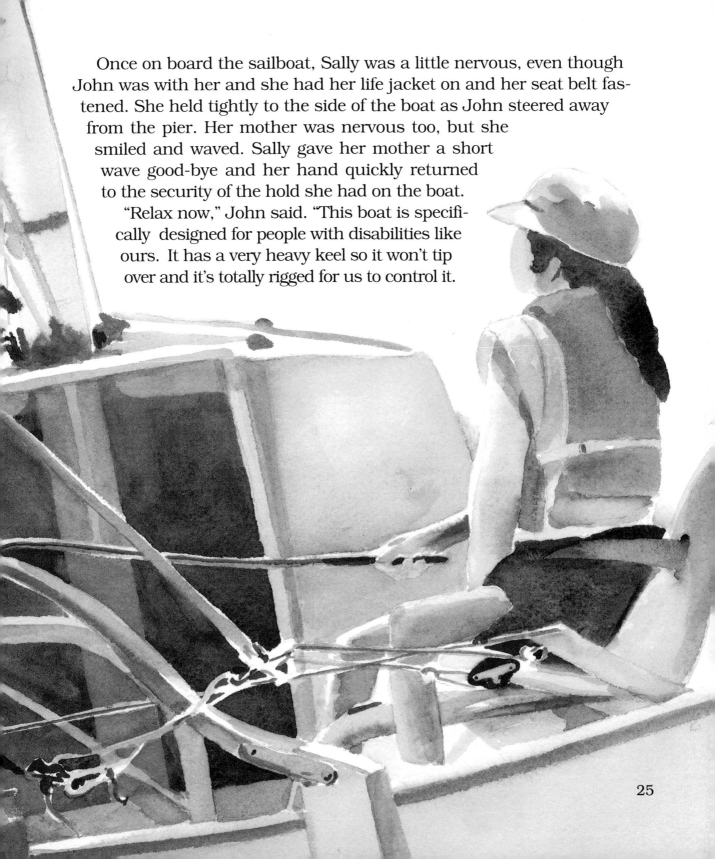

"Let's go out there and pretend to race some of the other boats. I know you're a very good racer."

"I used to be, but not anymore. Not since the accident. Someone else will win the big race in a couple of weeks, not me," she responded sadly.

"Ah, don't be so sure," John said. "Even though you had an accident, which was a major inconvenience, you'll see that you can still race with the best of them! Let's go!"

After sailing the inlet for a few minutes, John let Sally take the tiller and he helped with the lines. She felt more and more confident as she moved the little boat around the harbor.

The wind was perfect and the sailboat moved easily under Sally's control. The tiller had that familiar pulse of water passing by. Sally remembered this well. Suddenly she felt alive again and tears began to stream down her rosy red cheeks.

"It's okay, Sally," John said softly. "I cried the first time I sailed after my injury."

Sally looked back toward the shore where her mother and Tucker seemed smaller and smaller as the boat moved farther and farther away.

"And to think," she said to John, "we did the whole thing without help from anyone!"

John said happily, "I thought you said you couldn't sail anymore! I must have heard you wrong, judging by the way you're steering this boat." And they both laughed out loud.

As the weeks passed and the big race weekend approached, Sally sailed regularly with John. Her mother had a difficult time getting her interested in anything else and she never spent time sitting, overlooking the harbor and the boats below. She spent all of her time on the water learning racing techniques from John aboard the boat designed and built for sailors with physical disabilities.

One afternoon a few days before the big race weekend, she and John were sailing their course when two boys passed by. "We've been watching you, Sally," one yelled. "We can't believe you're sailing that thing. It's a good thing you can't race Saturday. We'd hate to have to beat you!" And off they went.

"Oh well," Sally said. "I can't race Saturday, but at least we can take the boat out and watch, can't we, John?"

"Sure, we can sit out and watch the races. It'll beat sitting up on the hill watching them, won't it!" he responded.

Sally was up early Saturday morning. This was race weekend and the entire town, including all her friends, would be going down to the harbor for the day. There were games, plenty of food, and lots of races. This was the last event before school started and everyone loved the big race weekend. Sally wanted to get there early, so her mother joined in the rush to get out of the house. Tucker was excited too. He knew something was going on and he wanted to be there. He couldn't go on the boat but her mother promised Sally she would take him to the harbor with her.

Sally could see children and their parents clambering around their boats, making ready for the races.

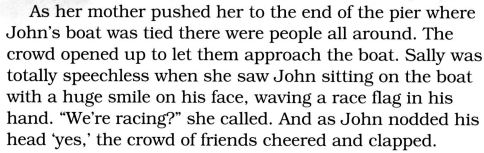

As her mother pushed her to the end of the pier where John's boat was tied there were people all around. The crowd opened up to let them approach the boat. Sally was totally speechless when she saw John sitting on the boat with a huge smile on his face, waving a race flag in his hand. "We're racing?" she called. And as John nodded his head 'yes,' the crowd of friends cheered and clapped.

"We're racing if you ever move onto the transfer box and get down here in the cockpit and start sailing this boat!" John yelled, laughing with excitement.

"Hold on, Sally," one of the boys said. "Don't you want to know the name of the boat you have entered in the race?" As the crowd moved away Sally could see the side of the boat and the name in big letters: *Broken Wings Will Fly.* She and her mother both started to cry with joy as they looked at the boat.

"Hey, are we going to get out of here and win a race or not?" John said as the crowd cheered again and Sally got aboard.

As they sailed off, Sally waved to her mother, Tucker, and her friends. And just as *Broken Wings Will Fly* approached the committee boat to check in for the race start, John pointed overhead and Sally looked up to see her little duck circle the harbor and then fly off over the trees. Sally smiled, turned to John, and said, "You never know what wonderful things can happen unless you try."

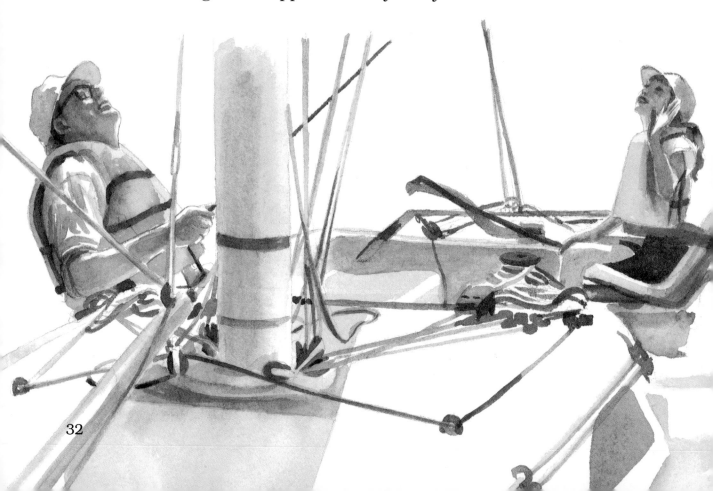